I0766464

The Book
of
Autumn

++++++++++

Billy Lou Silver

Give me the first six years of a child's life and you can have the rest.

RUDYARD KIPLING

Contents

Lucy Pearle
& The Ivybridge Tree

"It' s a childish tale,"
Said Abigail,
Lucy's older sister.
She'd been down to the woods herself,
Where the miller's son had kissed her.

Until one day, he went away,
The miller's precious Lou.
No note or trace,
He just left the place.
Some said he'd joined a crew.

And then others said
That poor Louie is dead.
He'd crossed that moor too late.
A screaming sound
And a finger found
That said the Noogan was his fate.

"He's gone to set-sail,"
Whispered Abigail,
"Make his fortune on the sea.
And when he comes back,
With doubloons in his sack,
There'll be plenty there for three."

To Ivybridge
Where evening midge
Are caught by swooping swallow
Here Abigail in wooded vale,
Had taken Louie to a hollow

A sacred tree, said to be
Where lovers consummated
Or chant their name,
And make your claim,
For love reciprocated.

Now Lucy Pearle,
Romantic Girl
Had fallen for a boy.
But he was unaware
That she should so care.
His name was Lawrence Malloy.

An all-boys' school,
She'd hear them call,
As they walked on past her gate.
A little coy,
She'd watch that boy
And every day she'd wait.

So convinced was she
That he would be
The lover of her life,
To that tree
She went to see
If she could be his wife

So, Lucy Pearle,
Romantic girl
Set off there alone.
It was getting dark
When she heard a bark
From the house of Miller Malone.

A white ribbon she'd take
And an inscription she'd make
Carving it on that tree.
But something would follow
And hide in that hollow
And that was the end of Lucy.

When next morning broke
And gentle chimney smoke
Rose from the village baker,
Hunter and hound
On that moor found
A dilemma for the undertaker.

All the town's people grieved
Then ranted and seethed
To hunt that Noogan down.
But nothing was seen
Not a fig, not a bean,
But stories ran rife in the town.

After twelve months had passed,
That ship at last
Returned with a reasonable hoard.
But far from beguiled,
Was Abigail, now with child,
For Louie was never aboard.

After several years,
Those Noogan fears
Began to be forgotten,
Until one day,
While Abigail was away
Her child found something all rotten.

"It's the end of a search,"
Said a man from the church.
"It's the Miller's precious Lou!
And with one finger less
I'm inclined to guess that
Here we have a clue."

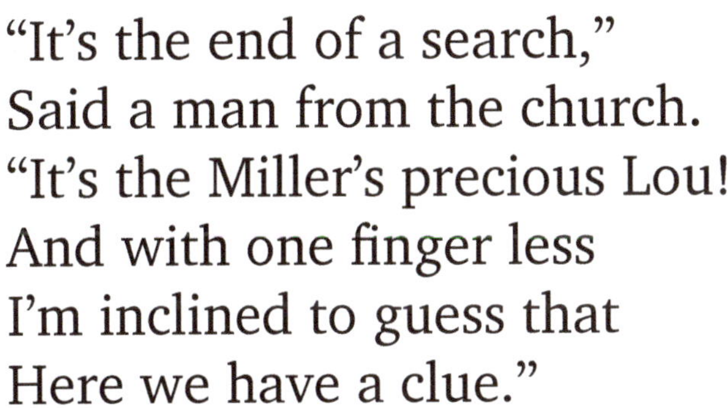

On Abigail's return
She would immediately learn
That questions for her abated.
And a pale Abigail
Looked suddenly frail.
It was a day she'd anticipated.

"That ring that she wore!"
Miller Malone swore,
"Louie before had been wearing."
And so Abigail
Began to wail
And confessed on a bible swearing.

"Yes, I took that ring back
By a meat cleavers hack
Then killed my Louie stone dead.
With his child inside
All the time he had lied.
He'd wanted my sister instead!

-But,...there's more to this tale,"
Wept Abigail
"My sister' s poor sorry fate.
To Ivybridge I would follow
And hide in that hollow
On that night she went out so late.

With wild jealousy
I read on that tree
The initials with whom she was smitten
And her life I would take
Was my grievous mistake
For 'L.M' were those initials written."

How could she have known
It wasn't Louie Malone
But initials of some other boy
And in her jealous confusion
Made a hasty conclusion
And denied Lucy forever from Lawrence Malloy.

To the gallows Abigail went
Trying to repent
Her daughter taken away.
"From that very first kiss,
How did it come to this?"
Were the last words Abigail would say.

Then when centuries went by
Two lovers would lie
Beneath a large old tree.
"How curious," the girl said
At the initials they read.
"Lucy Malloy? That's me."

Jack
CrippleSkip

ock your doors
And windows tight
Cos Jack CrippleSkip
Is out tonight

And those young children
Who dare to spy
Might see Jack CrippleSkip
Lurking nearby

Waiting and watching
For children who peep
So as to discover
Where they might sleep.

Where he lives
And where he goes
Nobody sees
And nobody knows

But you'll hear him come
To check the locks
Rattle the windows
And sometimes knocks

So close your curtains
Secure the latch
Or Jack CrippleSkip
A child he'll snatch.

With children collected
He steals them away
To squeeze out their essence
So some people say

Til mixed in tonic
Fizzy and black
Syrupy sweet
And bottled by Jack

We Moved
To A Valley Of
Witches

e moved to a valley of witches
When I was ten years old.
The property was cheap,
The cellar deep
And the reasons never told.

He was a pompous portly agent
Who pointed with his cane.
He talked and talked,
Around the garden walked
And there he would remain.

Mum pretended she was Country,
But was Towny through and through
(And dad), saw no wrong,
Just went along
'Cos he thought he could be too.

Little Jen was only four
And loved it like a child.
To Mum and Dad
Maybe just a fad
But were fools in places wild.

(Mum said) Country folk were friendly
With special country ways.
Now rubbished all the townsfolk
And just talked country praise

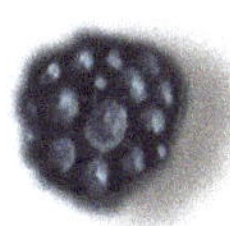

So, -there we were, picking fruit,
Blackberries for pies
When what I saw,
Tricked Newton's law
Witches in the skies!

Broomless crone, great rafts were flown
Loaded, ill-gotten gain.
Milking cows and squealing sows,
Bushels full of grain

None could see, how deviously
Worked this nest of wicked witches.
They had no idea,
As I point in fear
But laughed at me in stitches

Then overhead, I watched in dread
As a raft steered into view.
I caught her eye,
She'd caught a spy
But already it seemed she knew.

For loosed a punnet and I cried to shun it
Though mother was soon delighting.
Convinced was she,
Of country generosity
And sealed her fate by biting.

You would never believe,
This power to weave
As she feasted like a bear.
Smeared in pulp,
She'd gorge and gulp
And roared she would not share.

By setting sun,
Dark deed was done
My mother fell asleep
She barely woke
And barely spoke
No more interest did she keep.

When autumn neared,
My father feared
No more could he do
As she mumbled and stared
And no more she cared
Or slept the whole day through

Then...in stormy November,
A night I'll remember
Found mother sweeping the house.
Strange rhymes she repeated,
Then father she greeted.
An all-recovered spouse.

But I knew, I knew,
This wasn't true
This was something other.
Before me stood
No earthly good.
This was not my mother.

My father was fooled
Of who over him ruled
Though foul and uncouth were her ways.
Swore she did now
And ate like a sow
While all he could do was gaze.

But those eyes, those eyes,
I'd recognise
She knew we'd met before.
This cronish deceit,
Her spellwork complete
Somehow she'd crossed our door.

That night rolling thunder,
My bed I hid under
I knew she'd something to say.
Then door handle turned,
While black candle burned
Her footsteps proceeded my way.

"The dye is set,
You will forget
Or sicken your sister and you.
This home was mine,
Three fold to 9.
What's done cannot undo."

But that night I would dream
Of breathy steam
Rising from our cellar.
This impostor was feeding,
On my mum she was needing
Until she could expel her.

To the cellar I crept
While everyone slept
Still in my dressing gown
And soon would discover,
Small stairs to another
Leading me further down

Whispering air
Would lead me to where
A witch's door be found.
There, dripping stones
And rotting bones,
That chamber underground

And somewhere there hidden
Lay mother hex ridden
Last breaths ebbing away.
I was next to be stricken
And Jen she would sicken
If I did not act the next day.

How could it be broken,
This curse she had spoken
Reverse this life leeching spell.
Too canny, too clever
She knew it was never.
But something I could tell.

See witches I could,
And use it I should
To bring this crone her demise.
No time did I waste,
All witches were traced
To a place forbidden of eyes.

There, they auctioned their bounty
To some from the county
All types of well-to-do.
Councillors and masters,
Lawyers and pastors,
I could hardly believe it true.

And then there in the crowd,
A man bidding loud
The fat agent who sold us our place.
And what he greedily collected,
I'd never've suspected
Undergarments of lace.

By a hedge in a field
Was further revealed
As he tried them on for size.
While darting glances,
He worried at chances
Of someone's peeping eyes.

At his door that night,
His face turned white
As I told him all that I knew
And how his secret attire
Cost a witch at our fire.
Now something he should do.

His pride would now crumble,
Became weak and humble
And cried that I should not tell.
He'd known it was wrong,
Fooled himself all along
And would try, help break this spell.

She was Morag McGinty,
Aged one hundred and twenty
Devious to behold.
But it was Emily Crow,
Her earthly foe
That caused her house to be sold.

Morag before,
Had crossed the door
In the home of Emily Crow.
That same old jiggery
Hid her manners of piggery
As Morag began to sow.

But of Emily Crow,
She did not know
Was of witching ancestry
And failed at inducing
A coma producing
Until fatality

What Emily did next,
We still remain vexed
For Morag fled from this Isle.
But when the Crows moved north,
Old Morag came forth,
Some say from a witches trial.

No forwarding address,
The Agent confessed
The Crows had left behind.
The die was casting.
No time was lasting
The Crows... we had to find.

So ads he would run,
In every one
All northern publications
And who knows, who knows
Maybe the Crows
Will defy our expectations

(The advertisement read)
If you know Emily Crow
Of the southern valley
Urgent request, Morag addressed
And tell her not to tarry.

But as that night drew in
Morag flew in-
A rage, cursing me with bile.
Then Jenny she twisted,
As Morag insisted
Jenny'd be dead in a while.

And as things turned bad,
My silly old dad
Continued his silly old gaze.
I was down on the floor (when suddenly)
A knock at the door
Would change the rest of my days.

At my dad she screamed,
But to late it seemed
For the door was opened wide.
Her toxic grief,
Now disbelief
As a woman stepped inside.

Before next words were spoken,
Morag was broken
Contorting from head to toe.
And all brought about,
There was no doubt-
That this... was Emily Crow.

"I spared you before,
You've broken our lore
-Out! you will be driven!
All harm that you've made-
9 fold be repaid.
Til then, death not you be given."

And Morag McGinty,
One hundred and twenty
Shrivelled before our eyes.
All toothless and craggy
All crooked and saggy
Beneath an image of lies.

Dad was sick on the table,
Said, " I'm not quite able-
To see how that crone could will me."
And still shook his head,
Said, " I took It to bed..
Your mother's gonna kill me."

Mum doesn't remember
Much after September,
We found her concealed down below.
Her hair had turned white,
Otherwise all alright
Thanks to Mrs. Emily Crow.

So we packed up the car
And drove somewhere far-
More suitable to be.
And how did she know,
Mrs Emily Crow
To come so immediately?

"You see?, Don't you see?"
She whispered to me,
"The connection always remains.
You've ancestry.
We're family.
My blood runs in your veins."

Claims there have been,
That Morag's been seen
Still wayfaring country lanes.
From western coast
To southern most
To Bodmin's moorland plains.

But others contest
That the Agent confessed
She's in that chamber sealed.
He refused to sell
That house 'til he fell-
Dead, his diary revealed.

So readers take heed.
Think twice indeed
When below you comes a knocking.
It could be a bird or a bat,
A mouse or a rat
Or a canny witch you're unlocking.

and then there's the story about the
Crow, the Spider and the Beetle...

SPIDER'S LAMENT

"Oh," lamented spider
From the web that he had cast.
"Not a single bloody fly
And all this time has passed.

Look at all my workmanship,
Every loop support and brace.
I sat, designed and planned it all,
Like the finest bloody lace.

I charted out the north east wind
That passes for this way.
I set my web accordingly,
For every fly to stray.

I suppose all that's left to do,
Take down and pack away.
What's the use of all this artistry
If it doesn't serve to pay?"

"I overheard yer plans-
To take down and pack away,"
Said a bumbling little beetle
Passing along that way.

"I admire much the skill yer 'ave,
But it'll only go t' waste,
Without the skill of patience
And decisions made in haste."

"Yes thank you little beetle,
But I really know what's best
After all, I'm professional
And know a tad more than the rest."

"Lovely web. You're packing up?
Is that what I heard?"
Came a voice in the branches.
It was crow, the wily bird.

Spider replied with a nod
As he went about his task.
Wily crow thought carefully
"Would you sell it may I ask?

I could use the silk you see,
My nest needs some repair
And your fly desire, I require
For I have plenty there."

Crow then hopped away.
"I've another web to view.
That spider there, is keen to share
The kind deal I've offered you."

"Ok," agreed the spider.
Crow took the silk away
And promised that he'd be back
Before the end of day.

So was waiting spider
When beetle wandered by.
"I've sold my web," he proudly said
And beetle gave a sigh.

"You wouldn't wait with that web
That you'd made so very well.
But now you'll wait willingly
On those words that crow would tell.

Your time is short and you must leave,
Forget about that deal."
But spider ignored what beetle implored.
Spider was owed a meal.

"Hello there spider," said the wily crow
"You must be rather hungry.
On my beak, let's go."

But at that lofty nest
Spider saw no flies,
Just twiggy sticks,
Three hungry chicks
And a crow who told him lies.

The Perfect Shore

Through smoke of cigar,
At the end of the bar,
His presence every night.
Quietly drinking
Quietly thinking,
Sinking his thoughts out of sight.

The whisky soaked lugger,
That briny old bugger
Would morning sun set sail.
And for the price of drink
He'd change how I think
As he began to tell me his tale

That four sheeted skipper,
Was no day-tripper
But a sailor of seven seas
-Til a storm left him battered
And his ship mates were scattered,
Sea water up to his knees.

Abandoned alone
Lost and wind blown,
A captain without a crew.
No rudder, no mast,
He was the last
And knew his days were few.

Parched and delirious
His state became serious
And made final words to his maker.
But his soul's introspection
Found a paltry collection
Due to the deep blue undertaker.

"To the lovers I've promised,
To good friends-dishonest
To the hopes of all others deserving.
To the dreams I've snuffed out
By my ego- puffed out
Selfish, jealousy serving.

I'm a man who fell short
This, my final report
On love- I turned my back."
Then faded to dark
While his lost lonely barque...
Lit golden, rising from black.

It was not the sound
Of running aground
But the smell of corn cakes cooking.
Then laughter he heard
And a calling seabird.
To the bridge he frailly went looking.

"An island it seemed,
As I could not have dreamed.
All lush, mountains and mists.
From wide sweeping sands.
I saw waving hands.
-It's true," the captain insists.

"There, smiling faces,
Then friendly embraces
As if I'd been expected."
How shaking he stepped
Then gratefully wept.
"Like family I was collected."

Of that place and his days
He seldom says
But calls it The Perfect Shore.
"If each day is a measure
Filled mostly with pleasure,
Then work is work no more."

His blessings were crowned
When a woman he found
Who'd love him for forever.
"How could it have been
That she had seen
The man that I had never?

How perfectly
She belonged to me.
We could not come undone.
But I knew my worth
Was like sand to the earth,
Like a candle to her sun."

Says the drunken old salt,
"There's something at fault
When heaven's grace be given."
Then drains his drink
And begins to think.
"Must to its end always be driven?"

Oh happy life
Hand in hand with wife
Telling her his stories
Of former days
And drunken ways.
A braggart's former glories.

Pay heed, pay heed
For it's here as you read
Another storm arises.
The braggart, the drink
Leads not where they think
No matter who advises.

"Just a little tipple.
I'm sure my ship'll
Get me there and here.
See old faces again,
A chance to explain
Over a jug of beer."

When anchor was dropped
In the tavern he stopped
And started to exclaim
Of his amazing return
But would sadly then learn
No one remembered his name.

And so there he sits
Broken in bits
Talking of yesterday.
Once lovers beach walking,
Now stuck here slurred talking
Growing old lonely and grey.

And as each year goes by
He sets out to try
Find his island-wife once more.
But in an ocean of forever
He has never never never
Found that Perfect Shore.

The Tale Of Old Blac

From across that twigh-lit summer's moor
One evening knocking at his door
Disturbed the sounds of gentle snore
They both had met once before

Knew all too well, Sibelius Blacwin.

"Think I not know your every home?
Though to every corner do you roam.
No sanctuary for you in steeple or dome
'Be ever engaged', warned Saint Jerome?"

So was told Sibelius Blacwin

"The pleading scholar who'd asked for more.
Who'd once come knocking at my very own door
What was promised, you could not ignore.
The years burned bright were twenty four

And the candle is now low, Sibelius Blacwin.

Did I not keep my bargain's end?
And for your bidding, a demon send?
All your wants and desires given?
All your enemies from your path driven?

Is this signature not yours, Sibelius Blacwin?"

Twenty four years past, that very week
Was an ambitious young man with truth to seek.
But granting access to burning desires
Was the quest for truth consumed by its fires

So was the fate of Sibelius Blacwin

Studious scholar in tireless pursuit
Seeking that which has no refute
But the alchemist's quest has many a route
And after many long years still remained mute-

So had complained Sibelius Blacwin.

Revelation by hook or by crook
To the forbidden arts would Sibelius look
Monosencis and the Shadows Book
To transcribe, to borrow and sometimes took.

Like this, sowed Sibelius Blacwin

Then nefarious requisites eventually met
Signed with his blood, the contract set.
Keys to the world Sibelius would get
And twenty four years to pay his debt.-

The soul of Sibelius Blacwin

And soon enough gossip would spread
Of a man who raised life from the dead,
Walked across water and thousands fed.
"I can do more than Christ!" the Doctor said

The amazing Dr.Blacwin.

But golden was his own path paved
And adoration what he really craved.
The seers eyes grew ever depraved
Objects of desire, duly enslaved

The shameless Dr. Blacwin.

But when twenty-four years was drawing near
Sibelius felt dread and uncontrollable fear.
He scoured old texts and sought out the wise
But all said the same,-It would be his demise.

The reap of Sibelius Blacwin

To the church he repented, claimed Christ to extol
Then pleaded and begged they pray for his soul.
Their priests most high said they'd do all they could
But it was now up to him to try and do good.

How he cried, Sibelius Blacwin.

Sibelius Blacwin was a shrewd old man.
Insurance guards a second plan.
A lifetime's study had revealed curious mention
Of a world as ours in another dimension

And who has dominion over this earth?
And in another, has his contract still worth?
Could Sibelius save his soul?
Could he conjure such a hole?

Could it be done, Sibelius Blacwin?

Come the waning of that final year
Sibelius' escape was drawing near
When a villager's daughter fell gravely sick
And the priest had asked that Sibelius come quick.

So off went Dr. Sibelius Blacwin

Sibelius did good as best he could
And within an hour the child stood.
Right as rain and in goodly humour
Sibelius somehow had dissolved her tumour

The remarkable Doctor Blacwin

The thankful parents were amazed.
But in the village, questions were raised
Demanding answers from the church
Outraged parishioners would mount a search

To find Sibelius Blacwin

The Doctor, they claimed had hexed her grave
For the purpose of a life to save.
They swore that he would have no haven
While chuckled darkly a lofty raven

As they head for the house of Sibelius Blacwin

The Doctor was hauled from his door,
Up the path and across the moor
To a hill where an elder tree grows
There met his end with twitching toes.

The fate of Sibelius Blacwin.

The Book of Autumn   by Billy Lou Silver
MMXVIII

Contact.

billylousilver@mail.com

https://www.facebook.com/blsstories